This book is due on the last date stamped below. Failure to return books on the date due may result in assessment of overdue fees.

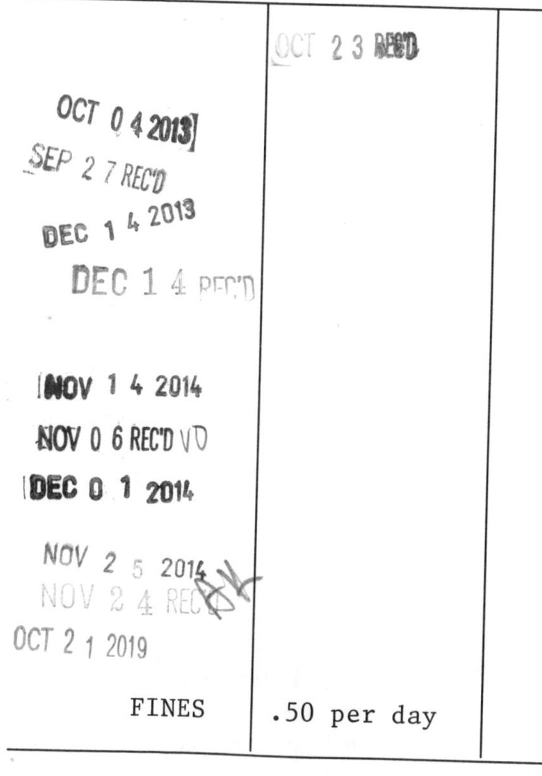

First
Grade
King

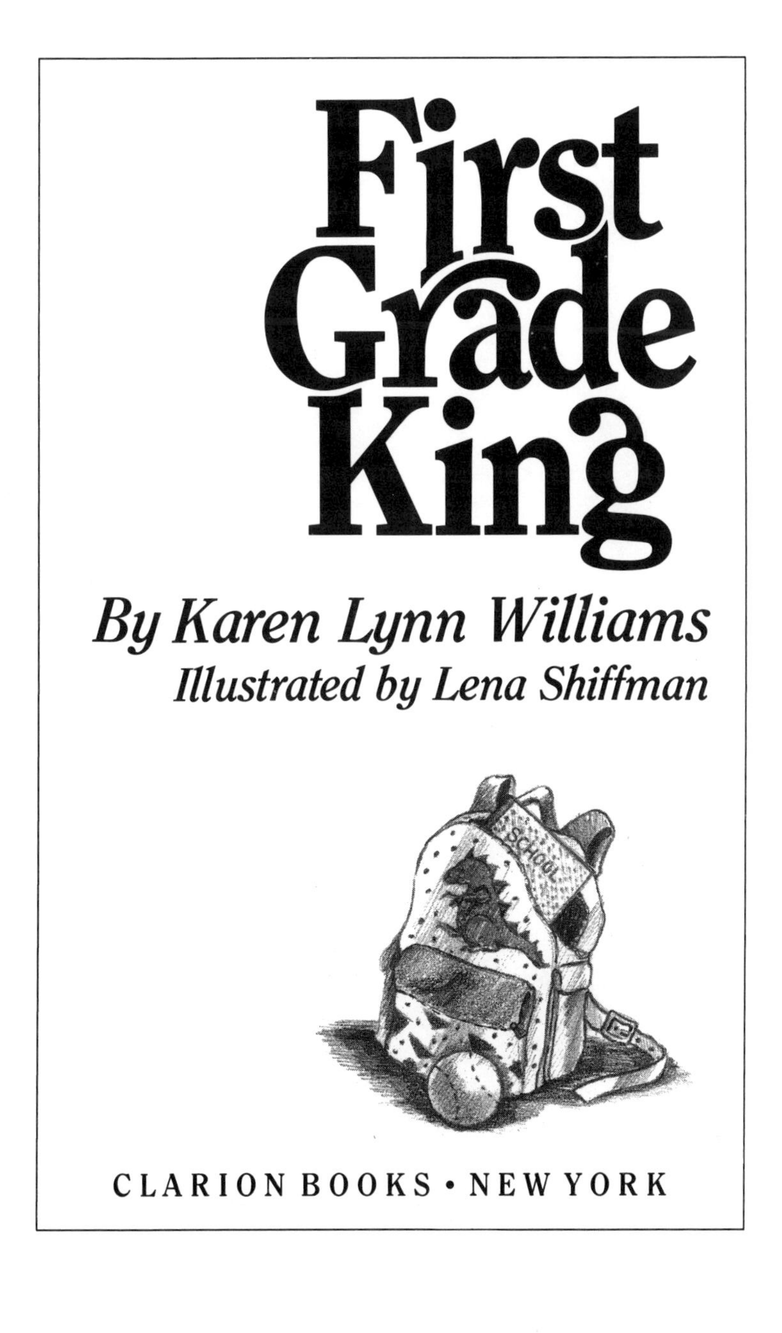

First Grade King

By Karen Lynn Williams
Illustrated by Lena Shiffman

CLARION BOOKS • NEW YORK

Clarion Books
a Houghton Mifflin Company imprint
215 Park Avenue South, New York, NY 10003

Printed in the U.S.A.

Library of Congress Cataloging-in-Publication Data

Williams, Karen Lynn.
First grade king / by Karen Lynn Williams; illustrated by Lena Shiffman.
p. cm.
Summary: Relates the experiences first-grader Joey King has at school: making friends, learning to read, and dealing with the class bully.
ISBN 0-395-58583-X
[1. Schools—Fiction. 2. Bullies—Fiction.] I. Shiffman, Lena, ill. II. Title.
PZ7.W66655Fi 1992 91-19474
[E]—dc20 CIP AC

VB 10 9 8 7 6 5 4 3 2 1

For Christopher, whose ideas helped.

First
Grade
King

Chapter
•1•

Joey King's eyes popped open. A pale gray light was sneaking in around the window shades. First day of first grade, Joey thought, and he sat straight up in bed. Time to get up.

He made his bed without even getting out of it. First he pulled the bedspread up over all the covers. Then he crawled onto the smooth part and pushed the spread over the pillow. Done. It was great sleeping on the top bunk. No one ever sent you back to make your bed over.

Joey hung upside down over the side of the bunk and made bug eyes at his brother. Daniel was starting third grade today.

"Hey, Dan," Joey whispered loudly. "Wake up."

No answer. Still asleep. No, pretending, Joey thought. He felt the blood rush to his head. His eyes felt like they would pop. Joey sat back up. Then he climbed down two steps of the ladder and jumped to the floor. *Thump.*

"Cut that out," Daniel growled from under the covers.

Joey did a little hop, first one foot, then the other. More thumping. Daniel really hated thumping.

"First day of school. Better get dressed," Joey told his brother.

Daniel rolled over and looked at the clock. He groaned. "It's only six thirty," he said. "Go back to bed."

Joey pulled the covers off his brother. "You have to walk me, remember? I don't want to be late."

Daniel grabbed the covers back. "Beat it," he said, "or you can walk alone."

"Mom said you have to walk me," Joey told his brother.

Last year Joey had been in kindergarten. His mother had walked him. Kindergarten was for babies. This year he would walk with Daniel. He was afraid to walk alone, but he wasn't going to be the only kid in the first grade who walked with his mom.

Joey started getting dressed. He put on his new blue jeans and long-sleeved striped shirt. They were new for the first day of school. He had new sneakers too. They had wild designs all over, just like Daniel's. Daniel wouldn't let him get the same color but they were close.

Joey went downstairs. He got all his stuff together. This year he had a backpack for homework and he had a lunch, just like Daniel. He was going to eat lunch in school and play with Daniel and his friends on the playground.

Joey looked at the clock in the living room. Seven, zero, zero. He waited for the numbers to change. Seven, zero, one. One minute. One minute was too long. Joey had just learned how to tell time, and he knew he still had to wait a whole hour.

Mom came downstairs. "I see you're ready for your big day," she said. She gave Joey an extra long hug and then began making breakfast.

"French toast and hot chocolate, special for the first day of first grade," she announced.

It smelled great, Joey thought. But then his stomach started to twist up inside.

"This is almost ready," Mom said. "Better run up and tell Daniel. He might want a few extra minutes on the first day."

Joey ran back upstairs. What if they were late? Late on the first day? Dad had already left for work and Daniel wasn't even up.

"Breakfast," Joey called at the lump in the bottom bunk. "Mom says get up, *now.*" Joey knew that wasn't exactly what Mom had said but he thought that was what she should have said. He pulled out Daniel's drawer. "Come on, Dan, you have to get dressed." The drawer came out fast. Too fast. One end fell on the floor. Thump again. Daniel moaned.

Joey started pulling out Daniel's clothes, looking for his new first day jeans.

"Hey, what are you doing?" Daniel was awake now. "Get out of my drawer." He jumped halfway across the room, ready to grab Joey. Joey ran out the door and down the stairs. At least Daniel was up.

Joey sat down at the table and squeezed syrup on his French toast. He made a design. JK for Joey King. He already knew how to write his name. This year he would learn

PLANET

how to read. Then Joey was going to read all those mystery and science books that Daniel read. He couldn't wait.

Joey looked at the French toast with the JK spreading out all over it. French toast was his favorite. He watched the butter melt in a little pool under the syrup. His stomach was twisting inside again. There was a place on the edge of the toast where the egg wasn't all cooked. It was the slimy white part.

Joey pushed his plate away. He wasn't hungry and Daniel still wasn't down yet.

"What's the matter?" Mom asked.

"Can't eat," Joey told her.

"First-day jitters," Mom said. She smiled. "I get them too. I still can't believe my baby's going to first grade. I'll miss you. Sure you don't want me to walk you?"

"No thanks," Joey mumbled. He hated it when Mom called him her baby. Joey figured he was still going to be the baby even when he was as big as Daniel. He didn't say anything today. He just let Mom hug him again.

"Try to eat a little," she said.

Joey ate a little. Then he put on his jacket and backpack. Daniel finally came down-stairs. He didn't have his shoes on. Joey watched his brother eat. He stuffed a whole half piece of French toast in his mouth at once. At least Daniel could eat fast. Joey felt sick. He went to the bathroom. What if Daniel had to go to the bathroom after eating all that food? He still had to brush his teeth and put on his shoes.

Joey looked in the mirror. A strand of hair stuck up from the top of his head, right in the middle. It looked dumb. He grabbed the fingernail scissors out of the drawer under the sink. Snip. He missed. Short pieces of hair slid down Joey's shoulder. Snip, snip. Got it. Joey brushed himself off and took a last check in the mirror. Then he stood up on the toilet seat so he could see his sneakers. Everything looked OK. Even his backpack looked clean and neat and new. It felt stiff but it looked great. Joey King was ready for first grade.

Chapter
• 2 •

Joey was waiting by the front door. "Come on, Daniel," he called.

Daniel finally came into the living room and put his backpack on. "Mom, why can't Joey walk by himself?" he said. "I want to walk with my friends."

Daniel never wanted Joey around when his friends were there. Joey thought if he had to walk alone, he might get lost and never get to school. Maybe the black dog on the corner would be out. His stomach twisted tighter. He could feel it in his throat. Maybe he should have let Mom walk him. Too late for that. She wasn't even dressed yet.

"Daniel," Mom said, "you can all walk together. You're Joey's brother. It's your responsibility." She gave Daniel a hug.

Daniel groaned. He walked out the front door, kicked a pebble, and followed it down the steps. "Come on, Joey. We'd better hurry or we'll be late."

Glad you finally figured it out, Joey thought. He ran after Daniel. He could see some more kids walking up ahead.

"Hey, Eddie," Daniel called to a friend at the corner. "Wait up."

"I see you got a babysitting job," Eddie said, when Daniel and Joey got to the corner.

"Kindergarten baby," someone called. Joey didn't know who it was.

"Think I'll meet you at school," Eddie said. He started to run ahead.

"I knew it," Daniel growled at Joey. "No one wants to walk with a baby."

Joey didn't answer. He saw more and more kids walking in groups as they got closer to Center School. They turned onto Dixwell Avenue and walked to the corner. Eddie and his friends were way ahead now. They crossed in the middle of the block.

Joey was glad Daniel went to the corner to cross, the way their mother always told them to.

Daniel and Joey met Brian at the light.

"Daniel, wait a minute and I'll walk with

you," Brian said. "I need to stay a few more minutes in case anyone else comes to cross." Brian was Daniel's best friend. He was a crossing guard. He wore an orange belt.

"Sure," Daniel told him. "We'll wait."

"We can't wait," Joey said to Daniel. "We'll be late."

Daniel rolled his eyes at Joey. "Go by yourself, then," he said.

Joey decided to wait. No one else came to cross. They were the last ones. Joey knew they would be late.

"OK," Brian finally said. "We can go." He and Daniel walked in front of Joey.

"Daniel," Joey called up to them. "Do you know which door I go in?"

"Of course." Daniel didn't even slow down.

"Who's your teacher?" Brian asked over his shoulder.

"Mrs. Fulks," Daniel answered for him.

Brian stopped to wait for Joey. Daniel stopped too.

"I had her. She's a great teacher," Brian said.

"Yeah," Daniel agreed. "That's what I told him."

"You're lucky," Brian said. "Mrs. Fulks is the best teacher I ever had. Maybe you'll make a papier-mâché eagle like we did."

"I remember Mrs. Fulks taught us bird calls," Daniel added.

Daniel and Brian were both laughing and making chicken noises when they came into the schoolyard. Joey laughed too. First grade was going to be fun.

Joey looked around the playground. There was Jeremy. And Rose. He knew them from kindergarten. Jeremy was with his mom. Rose was with her dad. Joey was glad he didn't have to walk with his mom. He felt grown up walking with Daniel and Brian.

Brrrrring! Joey jumped. It was the bell. Kids started rushing by him. They were yelling and laughing and talking. Joey started to run, calling, "Come on, Daniel." He was confused. Kids were running in all directions. He didn't know which door he was supposed to go in.

"That's just the first bell," Daniel said. He and Brian just kept walking and talking.

Now he was going to be late on the first

day of first grade, Joey thought. Just when things were looking good.

"You go that way." Daniel pointed to the steps leading up to two big blue doors. Now Joey remembered. The first graders used the blue doors.

"You can go by yourself now, can't you?" Daniel asked.

"Come on, Dan," Brian called.

Brian was waiting for Daniel. Joey wanted Daniel to come with him, but he didn't want to be a baby. "I know where to go," he said. Daniel and Brian disappeared around the corner of the building.

Joey got at the end of the line outside the blue doors. He wished he were in third grade like Daniel. Daniel always knew what to do. He had lots of friends and he didn't have to worry about anything. Third graders are lucky, Joey thought.

He took a deep breath and looked at the high wire fence around the schoolyard. It was the same fence he and Daniel used to climb for fun in the summer when they came to the playground. Daniel could climb all the way to the top. Joey could climb halfway. The fence had a new coat of paint.

The bell rang again. Joey felt like turning around and walking back the way he had come. But the line began to move, and Joey King was on his way into first grade.

Chapter
•3•

Joey looked up at the door monitor who held the heavy blue door open. She wore an orange belt and she looked big. Fourth and fifth graders were big. All the kids in the school were bigger than first graders, Joey thought, except kindergartners. But they didn't count.

Inside the school it was noisy and it smelled like school. The floor was shiny. The line turned left inside the door and headed down the hall. There was a teacher waiting at the door to the first grade classroom.

She had short blond hair and she was smiling. That must be Mrs. Fulks, Joey thought, and she's pretty.

"See if you can find your seats," the teacher said as everyone came into the room.

The first grade classroom was big. The walls were green and there were lots of pictures on them. Everything was neat and shiny and clean. There were real desks and every desk had a name on it in big neat black letters.

Some kids found their names and sat down. Joey looked for his name but he couldn't find it. He walked up and down two rows and looked at every empty desk. He only saw one J, but it wasn't for Joey.

He started up the third row. Still no more J's. Maybe he had made a mistake. Maybe he had missed his name.

Joey kept looking. J-O-E-Y, he kept spelling to himself, and then he saw it. JOEY KING. The second desk in the third row. He sat down and opened the top. Inside were two workbooks with his name on them. Joey took one out and flipped through the pages. They were brand new. No one had written in them. Joey put the books back in his desk. He took his special first day of school pencil out of his backpack. It had a fuzzy elephant on the end with eyes that jiggled. He put it on his desk.

The teacher came into the room and sat at her desk. She smiled. "Welcome to first grade," she said. "I am Mrs. Fulks, and I am very happy to have you all in my class. We are going to have a very exciting year in first grade."

Joey sat with his hands folded on his desk and smiled too. The desk in front of him was still empty. Joey liked being in the front. He was glad to be near Mrs. Fulks. She was wearing a pretty dress. It was blue and had flowers on it.

"When I call your name please raise your hand so we can all begin to get to know one another," Mrs. Fulks said. "Steven Atwood. Lisa Banner." Everyone looked around to find the person whose hand was raised.

"Ronald Boyd. Welcome to Center School," Mrs. Fulks said to the boy who raised his hand. "Ronald is new to our school," she told the class.

"Madeline Brenden." No one raised a hand. Mrs. Fulks made a mark in her book.

Then she called some more names. Joey knew some of the kids from kindergarten. Megan was there, and so was Christopher. He waved to Joey. Joey didn't wave back. He was waiting for his name.

"Joey King," Mrs. Fulks called. Joey raised his hand. "I know your brother Daniel," Mrs. Fulks said. "I'm very happy to have you in my class." Joey sat up straight and tall. He was glad Daniel was his big brother and had Mrs. Fulks first. Mrs. Fulks already knew who he was and he knew about first grade and making eagles and bird calls.

"King." Joey heard a whisper behind him. "Where's the queen?" Something poked him in the back, hard. It felt like a pencil. "Where's your crown?"

Mrs. Fulks kept calling names. Joey felt his face get hot. He knew it was getting red. He sat stiff in his seat. He didn't turn around. Something jabbed him again. "Hey, King, where's the prince?" The voice behind him laughed. It was Ronald. Ronald Boyd. The third name on the list, the big kid Mrs. Fulks had said was new in Center School.

Joey's eyes felt watery. What if Mrs. Fulks thought he was causing trouble? She might send him to the principal. She might tell Daniel his brother was a troublemaker. Joey wished Mrs. Fulks didn't know his brother.

No one had ever made fun of Joey's name before. He didn't like it. He wished his name weren't King.

Suddenly the classroom door opened. Mrs. Fulks looked up and smiled. "Come in," she said. Everyone turned around. Two girls stood at the door. "Hello, Molly," Mrs. Fulks said. "Is this your sister?" Mrs. Fulks looked down at her book. "Madeline?"

The bigger girl was Molly Brenden, one of Daniel's friends. "Yes," Molly said. "I'm sorry we're late. My mother said to tell you Madeline missed the special bus."

"I see," said Mrs. Fulks.

"I have to go," Molly said. She almost closed the door on her sister as she went out.

Madeline had lots of curly red hair and very big thick glasses. She walked right up to the front of the room. Mrs. Fulks was still smiling. "We're happy to have you in our class, Madeline," she said.

"I need to sit in the front," Madeline announced. Some kids laughed. Everyone was staring at Madeline.

Mrs. Fulks put her arm around Madeline's shoulders and led her to the seat in front of Joey. Joey wished Mrs. Fulks would put her arm around him. But he was glad he wasn't late on the first day of school. He was glad the whole class wasn't staring at him.

"Mad Madeline." Joey heard someone laugh, quietly, behind him. Ronald again. "Four-eyes," Ronald said. Mrs. Fulks didn't hear but Joey did. He wondered if Madeline had heard. She was putting things in her desk.

Mrs. Fulks finished reading all the names. Then she told about the classroom rules. "No running in the classroom or in the halls. We don't want anyone to get hurt. Be polite. Raise your hand when you want to talk."

Just like kindergarten, Joey thought.

"Homework must be neat and turned in on time," Mrs. Fulks continued.

Homework! Joey couldn't wait. In first grade he would have homework just like Daniel.

Finally, Mrs. Fulks said, "And if I'm ever absent, I want you to help the substitute. You can show her where the substitute file is. It will always be in my top drawer." Mrs. Fulks held up a red folder.

Joey didn't ever want to have a substitute. He hoped Mrs. Fulks would never get sick. Big people hardly ever got sick, Joey figured. He wondered if Mrs. Fulks was ever absent when Daniel had her.

Chapter
• 4 •

It was Friday. Joey was waiting for Daniel to get ready.

"Mom," Daniel called. "Where's my *Lion, Witch and the Wardrobe* book?"

Joey looked at Daniel's backpack. It was full of books—a reading book, a math book, a language arts book. He also had two joke books in there, Joey knew.

"Looks like you've got enough books, Daniel," he said. "Let's go."

"I need that book to read during free time," Daniel said from inside his closet, where he was looking under all the shoes.

Joey felt his own backpack. He didn't have one single book for homework yet. Just two pages. One for handwriting and one for math. Cinchy stuff. He could do it in five minutes. The first week of first grade was almost over and they hadn't even learned how to read. Joey was disappointed. Reading was the only reason he went to school.

Good thing tomorrow is Saturday, Joey thought. At least maybe he'd feel like eating breakfast again. Pancakes, maybe.

Everything was different in first grade. They didn't have any morning snack and no playtime. Ronald Boyd kept poking Joey in the back and calling him King and King Kong. Thinking about it made Joey's stomach hurt.

Daniel was lucky. He didn't care what kids said. He had a friend to walk to school with and he was in third grade. He got to do real homework and he could read just about any book he wanted to. It wasn't fair.

Joey stuck his foot under the bed until it hit something. He slid it out with his toe. "Here's your book," he told Daniel.

"Thanks," Daniel said, picking up the book. "Let's go. We'll be late."

Joey stopped to give Mom an extra hug and ran out the door after Daniel. "Hey, wait up," he said. Daniel took his time getting ready, but he sure could move fast when he wanted to.

"Hey, King," someone called from across the street. "Still got the little prince with you?"

"Knock it off, Eddie," Daniel called back. Daniel acted like he didn't care about the teasing. Joey wished he could act like that.

"I'm going to tell Dad they tease us," Joey said to Daniel.

"Are you kidding? Don't you dare." Daniel stopped short. Joey stopped too. "Listen, Joey, a tattletale is about the worst thing you could be. You tell on a kid for something like that and you really will have trouble."

"Doesn't it bother you when he says that stuff?"

"Eddie likes to act tough. He's just fooling around."

Joey didn't think it was funny. He hated it. Why couldn't they have a normal name, Joey thought. Like Brenden or Boyd or anyone else in his class. He ran to catch up with Daniel.

Brian was waiting for them at the next corner. Daniel went ahead with Brian and

Joey walked behind them. He knew Ronald would be waiting in the schoolyard to tease him. "Hey, King, where's your crown?" he'd say. He'd hold up four fingers behind his head like the points of a crown and do a silly little dance. Everyone would laugh. Joey hoped Ronald wouldn't see him. He wished Ronald would be absent for a change.

Joey went over to the door where his class lined up. He sat by himself on the steps and waited for Christopher. Ronald hadn't noticed him. He was busy.

"Want to see something funny?" Ronald was asking a couple of the kids. "Watch this." He held up something. Joey could see it was a nickel. Then Ronald walked over to Madeline.

"Hey, Madeline, if you can tell me what this is, you can keep it," he said. He held the nickel up pinched between his thumb and finger.

"Let me see," Madeline said. She squinted her eyes behind her glasses and put her face up real close to Ronald's hand. Some kids snickered.

"Hmmm," she said. "It looks like money."

"Sure it's money," Ronald said. "What kind of money? A dime? A quarter?" Everyone laughed. There were some big kids there. They were laughing too.

Madeline reached out her hand to take the coin.

"No way," Ronald said. "How much?"

"I have to feel it to tell," Madeline told him.

"No fair," Ronald said. "Ha, ha, you lose." He put the nickel back into his pocket.

Joey couldn't believe it. Madeline couldn't even tell which coin was which unless she felt it.

A few kids were still laughing. "Can't you even see? Your glasses are thick enough," someone said. Madeline just walked away. Ronald sure was mean. Joey felt embarrassed for Madeline.

He stood up to get ready for lining up. Madeline walked slowly over to where he was by the door. She didn't say anything. Maybe she thought he was one of the kids who had laughed. Joey felt bad.

"Hi," he said.

Madeline turned toward him. She put her

face up close to his. Joey had never seen such thick glasses.

"You're Joey King, aren't you?" Madeline asked.

Joey felt better. At least she could see him. "Yeah," he said.

"My sister, Molly, knows your brother."

"Yeah," Joey said again.

Then the bell rang and everyone lined up. Joey stood quietly behind Madeline.

Mrs. Fulks took the attendance. Then she said, "This morning it is our turn for art. You will all go to Mr. Russell's room."

Joey liked art. He liked to draw. His monster pictures were almost as good as Daniel's, with fangs and tilted eyes that looked evil. But now it was reading time, and they were going to art. How would he learn to read, Joey wondered. And why did they have to change everything around every day? One day was music, another day was gym. Joey didn't like new things. He liked things to stay the same. He liked to stay with Mrs. Fulks.

Mr. Russell, the art teacher, made everyone fold their hands while he talked. "I want you to understand that art is not playtime," he said. "We are here to work, just as in your other classes." He stopped and looked around the class. Joey lowered his eyes.

Out of the corner of one eye he saw Madeline next to him. She had her head bent so low she looked like she was praying. He figured Madeline wanted to disappear, just like he did.

Ronald's hand went up. The whole class looked at him. "Yes, Ronald," Mr. Russell said.

"Can I go to the bathroom?"

Mr. Russell was quiet for a minute, looking at Ronald. "You may go," he said finally, "but in the future you will remember that you are to use the toilet before you come to my class or after. I only see you once a week. It is a short time and there are too many of you for everyone to be going in and out. Is that clear?"

No one answered. But Joey figured Mr. Russell didn't want an answer. He just wanted to make sure no one used the toilet during art. Joey was sure glad he didn't have to go. He was sure glad tomorrow was Saturday.

When Joey got home from school, he ate an apple for a snack. Then he drank a big glass of orange juice. It tasted great. The first week of first grade was over. Two whole days without Ronald! Two days without special rules and getting to school on time and new teachers! Joey felt fine. He felt so good, he decided to set the table for dinner before Mom could ask him.

"Surprise," Joey said when Mom came into the kitchen to start dinner.

"Wow," Mom said. "First grade works wonders. The table is all set and I didn't even have to ask once." She hugged Joey.

"So," Dad said at dinner, "one week of first grade over. How does it feel to be a real scholar?" He reached over and pretended to examine Joey's eyes and ears. "You don't look any smarter," he teased.

Joey giggled. Then he said, "I still can't read."

"Give it a few more weeks," Dad said.

When everyone had finished eating, Daniel pushed his chair back from the table. "Friday," he said. He held his open hand out to Dad. "Don't forget my allowance."

Dad reached for his wallet. "Friday comes around too fast. How come you always forget your chores and never forget your allowance?"

"Joey sure remembered today," Mom said. "He set the table right after school, before I even asked."

Dad gave Daniel a dollar and fifty cents. Then he looked at Joey. "Let's see," he said. "First grade. I guess that means you need an allowance too." Dad gave Joey two quarters.

"Really?" Joey asked. "Every Friday? Thanks."

"Hey, wait a minute," Daniel said. "I never got an allowance in first grade."

"Circumstances change," Dad said. He winked at Joey. "We've got to consider inflation." Joey didn't know what inflation was, but he was sure glad Dad did.

Dad patted Daniel on the back. "Besides," he said, "I might consider a raise sometime soon. Right now I'd like to consider the apple pie I saw in the kitchen for dessert. Sulkers don't get any." Daniel sat up straight and made a crooked smile. Joey could tell he didn't mean it.

Joey's smile was real. A real allowance starting in first grade and apple pie for dessert! Joey hoped he could have seconds. He felt like he could eat the whole pie.

Chapter
• 5 •

Joey looked at the fried egg his mother had made for breakfast. Over easy. The way he liked it. Monday morning sure came fast. Who could eat on Monday morning with a whole week of school and Ronald? There were too many new things in school, too much to worry about. Carefully, Joey slid a half piece of toast out from under the egg. Plain with butter. Anything else would make him sick.

Then Joey remembered. Today was show and tell day. Daniel said Mrs. Fulks was the only teacher in the whole school who made time for show and tell. Mrs. Fulks was the best. Joey had a great show and tell. And today Mrs. Fulks was going to read some more of the Ramona book. She had read it to Daniel's class. Then Dad read the book to Joey and Daniel last year, a little bit every night. Joey couldn't wait to hear the next chapter even though he already knew what happened.

Joey looked at his plate. Maybe he could eat one egg.

Mrs. Fulks knew how a kid felt. "On Monday we need something special," she had said when she told them about show and tell.

Joey followed Daniel and Brian into the schoolyard and watched them disappear around the corner. He kept his hand in his pocket so he could feel his special rock, the one he'd brought for show and tell. It was hard and rough.

When Joey reached the first grade door, Christopher came over to him. "Hi," he said.

Joey liked Christopher. They sat together at lunch.

"Hi," Joey said.

"What did you bring for show and tell?" Christopher asked.

Joey had wanted to keep his show and tell a surprise. But he decided to show his rock to Christopher. He took it out of his pocket and held it in his hand so no one else could see.

"Hey, neat," Christopher said. "What kind is it?"

"It's granite," Joey told him.

"Those red things look like jewels."

"They're garnets," Joey explained. "I found them when we went camping last summer." He put the rock back in his pocket.

"Look what I brought." Christopher held up a large magnifying glass. It had a light on it.

"I have one of those," Joey said. "They're great."

The bell rang and the boys lined up with the rest of the first grade.

After she took attendance, Mrs. Fulks told the class to open their math books to page five. Ronald was making silly noises. Joey turned around. He saw Ronald tap Jonathan in the next row. Ronald pointed to Madeline and they both grinned. Ronald put his head right down to his book, the way Madeline was doing. They both laughed.

Joey thought about Madeline and her thick glasses. They were thicker than Christopher's magnifying glass.

Later on, when it was time to do board work, Madeline had to move up to a special seat next to the blackboard. Joey heard Ronald laugh again.

Joey thought that was mean. He thought about telling Mrs. Fulks. But Daniel said that was tattling. Joey couldn't be a tattletale.

"Now let's get on with show and tell," Mrs. Fulks said after lunch. Joey and his classmates cheered. They moved their desks into a circle and the show and tell person stood in the middle.

When it was Joey's turn, a lot of kids wanted to feel his rock. He got to pass it around the room. Madeline looked at it for an extra long time, holding it up close. "She takes too long," Emily complained.

The whole class had a turn, and then Mrs. Fulks announced that Madeline Brenden had a special show and tell, who would be arriving any minute. Just then there was a knock on the door, and a woman came into the room. She was pretty, with long dark hair. She had some papers and pictures and a chart with her.

"Madeline, would you please introduce our guest?" Mrs. Fulks said.

Madeline went to the middle of the circle. When she spoke, she seemed to be looking somewhere in the back of the room. In a very soft voice, she said, "This is Miss Gilbert, the school nurse, and she is going to tell you about my eye problem."

"Thank you, Madeline," said Miss Gilbert as she came to the middle of the circle. "I'm very happy to be here. This is a special class. You have a chance to learn about things very few first graders learn about."

She held up a poster. "This is a picture of the eye." It was orange and yellow with red and blue squiggly lines. It was kind of pretty, Joey thought, until you remembered it was an eyeball.

"Gross," Ronald whispered.

"This is the cornea or outer covering of the eyeball." Miss Gilbert pointed to it on the picture. "This is the lens, which focuses the light we see."

"Like a camera," Mary Jane said.

The Eye
Lens
Retina

"Right," said Miss Gilbert. "And back here is the retina. It's like a screen. The picture we see is formed there and sent to the brain."

Then Miss Gilbert held up a different picture. It was all orange with veins going through it. "This is a normal retina. But Madeline's retinas look like this." She held up another picture with black spots on the orange. "Madeline's retinas have scars on them."

"I have a scar where I got stitches." Jonathan showed the scar on his arm to the class.

"Yes, like that," Miss Gilbert said. "Because of the scars, Madeline's retinas do not send a complete picture to her brain."

Christopher raised his hand. "How did it happen?"

"Good question," Miss Gilbert said. "The doctors think that Madeline's mother had a disease when Madeline was a baby still growing inside her. She had the disease right at the time Madeline's eyes were developing. The doctors think this disease comes from poorly cooked meat."

"Can you catch it?" Ronald called out. Joey hadn't even thought about that. But he wondered what Miss Gilbert would say.

"No," she said with a smile. "This is something that only happens to a developing baby inside the mother. And it is very unusual."

"But Madeline wears glasses. Why does she have to get so close to the blackboard?" Mary Jane asked.

"Madeline wears very strong glasses to help her see. But even with the glasses, she does not see things the same way most people do." Miss Gilbert held up a sheet of paper with two pictures of a tree on it. One was clear, with all the leaves and branches showing. "This is the way most of us see a tree," Miss Gilbert said. Then she pointed to the other picture. "This is what the doctors think Madeline sees." It looked like a blurry, greenish ball on top of a brown pole.

Joey looked at Madeline. She was just staring at Miss Gilbert and her picture. He wondered what she was seeing. Was Miss Gilbert all blurry? Joey was glad he could see things the way they were. He was glad he didn't have to introduce the nurse and have everyone talk about his problems.

Mrs. Fulks thanked Miss Gilbert for coming. After the nurse left, the whole class was quiet. Even Ronald didn't have anything to say for a change. Joey wondered if they were all thinking about Madeline like he was.

They straightened out their desks. "And now I have a show and tell to share," Mrs. Fulks said. "I have two things to tell you. One is happy and the other is sad."

Joey liked being up front near his teacher. He wondered what she was going to say. He never heard of a teacher bringing show and tell before. He wished there wasn't a sad part.

"Tell us the happy one first," Jonathan said.

Joey remembered that Dad always said, save the best for last. "No, tell us the sad one first," Joey said.

"I'm feeling sad today," Mrs. Fulks said, "because my father is in the hospital. I got a phone call last night."

"What's wrong?" asked Madeline.

"He has a problem with his heart. It's kind

of scary. He lives far away." Mrs. Fulks looked worried. Joey knew he would be worried if his dad were in the hospital. Joey liked the way Mrs. Fulks always told them how she felt.

Joey felt bad. But then Mrs. Fulks smiled, and he felt better. "The happy part is, it's my birthday today," she went on.

"How old?" Ronald called out.

"I'm not telling." Mrs. Fulks laughed. "But I brought brownies to share."

The whole class cheered and said, "Happy birthday!"

"I'll read *Ramona* while we eat," Mrs. Fulks said.

Ramona and brownies, Joey thought. Maybe even Mondays in first grade would be OK.

Chapter
• 6 •

Tuesday morning. One day closer to Friday. Friday afternoon was still the best.

Joey looked at the soggy Cheerios floating in his bowl. On Saturday Cheerios looked great. But today, with four more days of Ronald left in the week, Cheerios didn't look so good. Even with sugar on them.

Joey took a spoonful of cereal, just a little one. Two Cheerios and milk. Too much milk. Some dribbled down his sweat shirt. He wiped it off with his napkin. Now there were two dark spots on his purple shirt.

Today was the first time Joey had worn this shirt. It was an old one of Daniel's, and Joey liked it. It had a black spider and a sparkly silver spider web on the back, and in the spider web it said "Help save our wild life," as if the spider had written it. Joey felt good in that shirt.

Daniel slurped up the last of the sugar milk in his bowl. At least someone was enjoying breakfast, Joey thought.

"Hey, that's my shirt." Daniel pointed at Joey. "Take it off."

"Mom put it in my drawer," Joey told him.

"Mom," Daniel called, "Joey has my shirt!"

"Daniel," Mom said, "that shirt is much too small for you. You never wear it anymore."

"I like that shirt. It's one of my favorites."

"Let Joey wear it for today. I'll put it back in your drawer after I wash it, if you want me to."

"I do," Daniel's voice sounded sulky.

"By the way," Mom added, "next week Daniel starts intramurals, so you boys won't be walking home together on Thursdays."

Joey had forgotten all about that. How would he get home on Thursdays? He didn't want to walk by himself. What if he forgot the way? "Can't I just wait for Daniel?" he asked.

"No," Mom said. "I was talking with Mrs. Brenden, and Madeline needs someone to walk home with. She's not taking the special bus anymore. It takes too long. She usually walks with Molly, but Molly will be staying for intramurals also. So I told their mother you would walk home with Madeline on Thursdays."

"Great," Daniel said. "Joey can walk with Madeline every day."

"Just on Thursdays, after school," Mom said.

"But, Mom," Joey told her, "Madeline can't see. She probably doesn't even know the way home."

"I'm sure she knows it just as well as you."

That's what Joey was afraid of. "You'll see," Mom said. "It won't be so bad. The first time is always the hardest."

"Hey," Daniel suggested. "Maybe you'll have to hold her hand. Joey has a girl friend, Joey has a girl friend." Daniel dodged past Joey and started up the stairs.

"You're just saying that because I get to wear your shirt," Joey told him. He went slowly up the stairs after Daniel. I hope

Ronald doesn't find out I'm walking home with a girl, he thought.

◇

When Joey walked over to get in line, Ronald was singing, "Here comes the king, here comes the king." Joey was just about the last one to arrive, so all the kids heard Ronald. He could feel his face burning.

A few kids snickered. Then a voice said, "You be quiet, Ronald Boyd." It was Madeline. She sounded like someone's mother, and she looked like she was talking to the air. "Mrs. Fulks said no teasing."

A few kids laughed again but Joey was impressed. He couldn't believe someone was actually telling Ronald off, and that someone was Madeline.

"Hey, four-eyes, Mrs. Fulks meant in school. Or can't you see we're still outside? Who are you, anyway? The queen or something? Looks like the king has a queen."

Madeline ignored Ronald and got into line. When the bell rang, she walked right into school like she didn't care what Ronald did or said. Madeline was OK, Joey thought. She was the only one who had stuck up for him. Maybe she would know the way home from school on Thursday. Joey just bet she would.

"Our reading lesson is a review from kindergarten," Mrs. Fulks announced. "Who remembers the snake sound?"

Betsey raised her hand first. "Ssssss." Betsey said it so loud she turned red. Joey heard Ronald laugh.

For once Joey agreed with Ronald. It was pretty funny, but worse, it was dumb, Joey thought. Dumb and boring. Why did they have to do kindergarten work? At this rate he was never going to learn to read.

Mrs. Fulks gave them directions. "Look at each picture and circle those with names that have the snake sound in them. Now I want to hear the whole class make a healthy snake sound."

"Sssssssssssss." Oh brother, Joey thought. Yuk. He could feel spray on the back of his neck. Ronald was making a juicy snake sound.

"Remember," Mrs. Fulks added, "the snake sound can be in the beginning, middle, or end of a word. Let's try a few together. Madeline, will you try number one, please?"

No one said a word. Madeline didn't say anything either.

"Madeline," Mrs. Fulks repeated, "does picture number one have the snake sound in it?" The whole class waited. Madeline had her head down, almost touching the page on her desk.

The answer is yes, Joey thought. Picture number one is a seal, and the snake sound is at the beginning. Joey kept his eyes on his paper. Come on, Madeline, answer yes. Come on.

Finally Madeline looked up. "I can't see what the picture is," she said in a soft voice.

"Can anyone help Madeline?" Mrs. Fulks asked. Lots of kids raised their hands. Joey raised his hand too. They all knew picture number one was a seal, but Madeline couldn't even see the picture, so how could she know?

Joey never wanted to be called on and not know the answer. That was one good thing about doing dumb old kindergarten work. At least he wouldn't make mistakes.

"It's a seal," Ronald called out before Mrs. Fulks could choose someone. "Anyone knows that."

"Seal is correct, Ronald, but next time please wait until I call on you."

"Hey, King, four-eyes doesn't even know what a seal is," Ronald whispered behind Joey. Joey heard him but Mrs. Fulks didn't. Maybe no one else heard either. Joey hoped Madeline didn't hear. He wondered if she felt bad about not being able to see the seal. Joey felt bad and Ronald made it worse.

Why did Ronald have to be in their class anyway? Without Ronald, first grade would be OK. If he could learn to read, and if his name weren't King, first grade would be great.

Chapter
• 7 •

That night after dinner, Joey was in his pajamas. He looked at the clock. Eight, zero, zero. Eight o'clock. Joey's bedtime. Dad was setting the table for breakfast. Joey hoped he wouldn't notice the time. Daniel was sitting at the table. He was still doing homework.

Daniel was lucky. He got to do homework. He got to stay up late.

Joey sat next to Daniel. He looked at the Cheerios box Dad had put on the table for breakfast. He saw a big C. He ran his finger under the big black word. C-H-E-E-R-I-O-S, he spelled to himself. Cheerios. Cheerios was a good name for cereal, Joey thought. Joey Cheerio. No, Cheerio wasn't a good name for him.

Joey wondered what other words were on the box. He tried spelling some of them out loud. "O-A-T. B-R-A-N."

"Cut that out," Daniel said. "I'm trying to work."

Joey knew how he could get Daniel to read the words for him. He pulled the bright yellow and blue box toward himself. "I'm reading this box," he said.

"You can't read," Daniel said.

"Can so," Joey told him.

"Prove it," Daniel said. "Read this word." He pointed to the O-A-T word. Joey just looked at him.

"See," said Daniel. "It says oat bran."

"Oh," Joey said. Joey Oat. Joey Bran. Joey Branoat, he tried.

"Made from the grain highest in protein." Daniel was still reading.

Joey Protein. Joey Grain. No, Joey thought, Cheerios words weren't good people names. But he had another idea. "Dad, can I stay up until eight thirty?" he asked.

"I think a big first grader can stay up an extra half hour," Dad said.

"Wow," Joey said. "Every night?"

"Sure," said Dad. "As long as Mom can still get you out of bed in the morning."

"That's not fair," Daniel said. "I had to wait until second grade to stay up that late."

"Everyone is a special case," Dad said. Mom and Dad always said that. Sometimes Joey didn't like to be a special case, but this time it was OK.

"You're a special case all right," Daniel said. He made a face at Joey.

Joey didn't care. He was going to use the extra time to learn how to read.

He got a piece of paper and started writing the words *Cheerios* and *Oat Bran,* just like on the Cheerios box. He made big neat letters. He liked the way they looked. Tomorrow he'd show his paper to Mrs. Fulks. Maybe she would hang it on the special work board. Joey could read the words to the class.

◇

On Wednesday morning Joey jumped out of bed. Getting up after staying up later was no problem. He felt great. Being in first grade was great. He was getting an allowance.

Fifty cents every week if he made his bed and set the table for dinner. Now he got to stay up a whole half hour later.

Joey put his extra work paper in his backpack. If he could stay up a half hour every night, Joey figured he could learn to read in no time. He couldn't wait to read his Cheerios words to Mrs. Fulks.

Joey followed Daniel and Brian into the playground. He didn't see Christopher. Ronald didn't seem to be around either.

Joey walked over to the big blue first grade doors. Madeline was there. She was standing straight and tall in front of the doors like she was in line. Joey leaned against the wall. He wished he had some chalk. He wanted to practice writing his new words on the blacktop.

Madeline turned around. "Mrs. Fulks is absent," she said without even saying hi.

"What do you mean?" he asked.

"She's not here today."

"Who?" Joey asked. His stomach started to twist up inside.

"Mrs. Fulks," Madeline said again. "She has to go to Cincinnati to see her father. He's sick. She has to take an airplane." Madeline sounded like she might cry. "She's going to stay a week, maybe even longer."

"How do you know?" Joey demanded. He felt angry. Madeline acted like she knew everything.

"My mother saw Mrs. Fulks in the grocery store. She was getting some things for her family before she left."

Joey knew Mrs. Fulks' father was sick. She had told them. But he didn't know a teacher could do that. Just leave school for a whole week even if her father was sick. It was probably illegal, Joey thought.

"I hope we don't get Mrs. Sullivan," said Madeline. "Molly says she's mean."

Mrs. Sullivan? Joey wondered what Madeline meant. Then he knew. A substitute. If Madeline was right, they were going to have a substitute. Maybe for a whole week or more. Now he wasn't going to be able to show Mrs. Fulks his Cheerios paper.

Kids started lining up behind Madeline. Madeline didn't tell anyone else about Mrs. Fulks. Neither did Joey. Maybe Madeline was wrong, he thought.

The bell rang. Joey closed his eyes tight for a minute and made a secret wish. "Please, oh, please, let Mrs. Fulks be here." He opened his eyes and followed Madeline into the school.

The wish didn't work. There was a stranger at Mrs. Fulks' desk. She was big and had short brown hair that was kind of frizzy.

Joey sat in his seat. He could hear whispering all over the classroom.

"Hello," the strange woman said after all the kids sat down. "My name is Mrs. Sullivan. Mrs. Fulks will be absent for a few days, and I will be your teacher. Mrs. Sullivan," she said again. "Please repeat after me."

"Mrs. Sullivan," Joey whispered.

"Before we begin, I want you to know I expect good behavior. I have made a chart." Mrs. Sullivan held up a piece of poster board with names and lines on it. "Every time someone misbehaves, they will get a check, so Mrs. Fulks will know who has been causing trouble in her absence." She taped the chart on the wall.

"Now I need to learn your names." Mrs. Sullivan began to read the class names. Her voice was kind of crackly. Joey waited for his name. He came after David Hull.

"King, Joey," Mrs. Sullivan said.

"Here." Joey could barely whisper.

"Where?" Mrs. Sullivan called loudly. "Speak up."

"That's the king," Ronald announced, pointing at Joey.

"Well," Mrs. Sullivan said, "Joey may be the king, but just remember, I make the rules." She stared at Joey. The whole class looked at Joey. Joey looked down at his desk.

Dumb name, he thought. Dumb Ronald. Joey felt awful. How could they do that to a kid? Give him the best teacher ever and then take her away? In kindergarten his teacher was only absent for one day. Sara's mom had taken care of the class. They had a special snack and played games. Joey wished he were still in kindergarten. He wished he could stay back.

If he were a repeater, Joey thought, he wouldn't have a substitute. If he were a repeater, Ronald wouldn't be in his class.

Chapter
• 8 •

Joey looked at the big clock over the classroom door. The big hand made a little jerk every time another minute passed but it barely moved. It seemed like they had a substitute for two days already, but it wasn't even lunchtime yet.

At least Mrs. Sullivan had the substitute folder, and she was doing everything the way Mrs. Fulks did. But a lot of kids were getting checks. Ronald kept leaving his seat without permission, and some of the others were talking out loud. They didn't do that when Mrs. Fulks was there. Joey was glad he didn't have any checks.

Mrs. Sullivan walked up and down the rows with her yardstick while they did their seat work. Joey wished she wouldn't do that. He wished Mrs. Fulks were there.

Mrs. Sullivan was getting closer to his desk. He looked down at his phonics paper. He was finished, but he pretended he was still working.

Mrs. Sullivan stopped right behind Joey. Joey couldn't see what she was doing. He almost stopped breathing and kept looking at his paper.

"Very nice printing," Mrs. Sullivan finally said. She patted Joey on the shoulder and walked by.

Joey started to breathe again. He looked at the clock. The big hand skipped again and then the clock made a low buzz. Eleven o'clock.

"Everyone put your books away and clear your desks," Mrs. Sullivan said.

What now? Joey wondered. They were supposed to do seat work until eleven thirty. Joey made mistakes telling time sometimes but he knew it wasn't eleven thirty yet. Mrs. Sullivan had the substitute folder. Why didn't she do things the way Mrs. Fulks told her to?

Joey hoped Mrs. Sullivan wasn't going to start being mean like Molly told Madeline.

Mrs. Sullivan put a black case on her desk. She opened it up and took something out. Some kids were stretching their necks and kneeling on their chairs to see what it was.

It was shiny and silver with some brown wood parts and a button.

"It's a harmonica," Sally said.

"No it's not. It's too big," Christopher told her.

That's what it is, Joey thought, a giant harmonica. A real one. Not those little toy ones you got at birthday parties and stuff.

Mrs. Sullivan didn't say anything. She just put the giant harmonica to her mouth and started to play. The music was loud and clear and it kind of quivered. Mrs. Sullivan moved the harmonica back and forth so fast, it sounded like there were two harmonicas playing, or maybe even three, Joey thought.

Mrs. Sullivan tapped her feet and some kids started clapping. Mrs. Sullivan nodded her head up and down and waved one hand. Joey knew she meant "Come on," and he started to clap too. The song was "Oh Susanna." Joey knew that one. He started tapping his feet. He could almost feel the music.

When the music stopped, the whole class started talking at once. "Play some more." "Where did you get it?" "How did you learn to play like that?"

"I learned when I was about your age," Mrs. Sullivan told them. "My father used to play, and he started teaching me when I was in first grade. I guess I taught myself, mostly. I got this harmonica at the music store."

Then Mrs. Sullivan started to play again. She walked up and down the rows, tapping her feet and rocking back and forth. Some of the songs Joey knew and some he didn't. Mrs. Sullivan told everyone to sing along if they knew the words. Even Ronald was singing. Not making trouble or anything.

Suddenly, Mrs. Sullivan stopped. Her face was red. "Get your lunches," she said, all out of breath. "We've nearly missed lunch. Line up."

Joey looked at the clock. Sure enough, the big hand and the little hand were both

stopher
Ro
Jo
Mac

pointing to the twelve. Joey thought it was funny how time never seemed to go at the same speed. It was always faster or slower than you wanted it to be. He wished Mrs. Sullivan would play some more.

Joey wished he could play the harmonica like that. Maybe he could learn. Mrs. Sullivan said she'd learned when she was in first grade. Joey couldn't believe Mrs. Sullivan was ever in first grade.

Madeline got in line behind Joey. "Looks like Molly is wrong about this substitute teacher," Joey told her.

"Wait until I tell her about Mrs. Sullivan's harmonica," Madeline agreed.

"Mrs. Sullivan, the musical substitute," Joey said. He liked that.

"But she still gives checks," Madeline said.

"I didn't get any," Joey told her. And he wasn't going to, either. Having Mrs. Sullivan for a substitute was going to be OK after all, Joey thought. When he went down the hall, he still felt like dancing.

Chapter
•9•

When Joey opened his lunch box, he found a special treat. It was a Milky Way bar. The tiny kind. Joey wanted to eat the Milky Way first, but he was supposed to eat his sandwich and fruit first.

Joey unwrapped his sandwich and spread out the paper. He put his milk and grapes and candy on the paper, like a placemat.

"Madeline has to smell her food to tell what it is." That was Ronald again. He was sitting almost across from Joey, two seats away from Madeline. All the kids at their table looked at Madeline. Joey looked too. She practically had her head inside her lunchbox. Not smelling it, Joey figured, just trying to see it.

Someone should do something about Ronald's big mouth, Joey thought.

While he was thinking about it, Joey picked up his sandwich. Before he could take a bite, he noticed his Milky Way was missing. He looked in his lunchbox. He looked under the table. Gone. His Milky Way was gone. Someone had taken it.

"Who took my candy bar?" he asked.

"Not me," Christopher said.

"Not me," Mary Jane said.

Jonathan looked under the table.

Ronald looked at Joey and smiled. He made a big toothy smile and made his eyes go up and down. Ronald took it, Joey thought. I'll bet he did.

He couldn't prove it, Joey knew. It was no use telling on Ronald. Ronald had probably eaten it already. There was nothing Joey could do.

"You can have some of my dessert," Christopher said. He handed Joey a cookie. "Chocolate chip."

"Thanks," Joey said, but he wasn't sure he could eat it. He didn't feel like eating his sandwich or his grapes, either. He didn't feel like being in first grade, or like having to go back to the classroom, even if the substitute wasn't mean. Joey wished Mrs. Fulks were here. Maybe he could go to the nurse. Maybe he was sick.

But Joey knew he couldn't go to the nurse. She'd know he wasn't sick, and she would just send him back to class. The whole class would look at him.

Joey followed the other kids out to the playground. The big kids were playing soccer. Joey wished he were a big kid instead of a first grader. He wished he were in third grade like Daniel. The big kids always got to the gym equipment first.

Joey and Christopher stuck together. They walked around the playground, keeping away from Ronald. It wasn't easy to hide on the playground. No one was allowed off the blacktop. It was against the rules to go near the bushes or up the steps or around the building.

"I brought a tennis ball," Christopher said, patting a bulge in his sweat shirt pocket.

"We could play keepaway," Joey suggested.

"Yeah," Christopher said, "but we'd need another person."

"Yeah," Joey agreed. He didn't feel much like playing, anyway.

Joey saw Madeline standing near the lunch aide. She was following Mrs. Warner wherever she went. "Let's go over by Mrs. Warner," he said.

But when they got there, Mrs. Warner was shooing Madeline away. "You kids go play," she said. "Run around and get some exercise. That's what you're out here for."

Joey, Christopher, and Madeline walked back toward the school building. Joey leaned against the wall.

"Now what?" Madeline asked.

Christopher started tossing his tennis ball against the wall.

"Neat," said Joey. "An orange tennis ball."

Christopher threw it at the wall again. The ball bounced on the ground and he caught it.

Madeline started to laugh. "That makes a funny sound," she said.

"It's kind of an old ball," Christopher said. "Soft. That's why my father gave it to me."

The ball hit the wall and the blacktop again. "Pong, thunk," Madeline said.

Joey laughed. "Pong, thunk," he repeated.

Christopher threw the ball again. "Pong," he called. Joey ran in front of Christopher. Before the ball could bounce, he caught it. "Thunk," he yelled.

Madeline and Christopher laughed. Joey threw the ball against the wall. "Pong," he called.

"Thunk," yelled Christopher, catching the ball before it bounced and before Madeline could catch it. "My turn."

"Right," Madeline said. "Let's make rules. If you throw the ball and you catch it, you get a thunk. If someone else catches it, they get the thunk and it's that person's turn."

"Sure." Joey and Christopher agreed.

"Hey, you little kids, watch out," Eddie called as the soccer ball rolled over toward them.

Christopher threw the tennis ball, calling "Pong" as Eddie ran in front of him. "Missed it," Christopher said. "Eddie got in my way."

"No thunk for you," Madeline said. "Let me try."

Madeline threw the ball against the wall as

she yelled, "Pong." The ball hit the blacktop and rolled over toward the soccer game.

"Oh no," Christopher said. "That's the end of my ball."

"I'll get it," said Madeline. She ran right into the middle of the big kids' game.

"Out of the way. No first graders allowed," one of them called. But Madeline kept going until she had the ball.

"No thunk for me," she said, running back to Joey and Christopher. "Joey's turn."

Joey took the ball. He was going to get a thunk and another turn. He knew just how hard and how high to throw it to make it bounce right where he could catch it.

"Pong."

"You first graders can't play here." That was Eddie's voice. *Thunk.* Eddie was in the way again. Joey missed.

"You don't own the schoolyard," Madeline told Eddie. She picked up the ball and handed it back to Joey. "You get another turn."

"Stay out of our way or else," Eddie warned them. He went back to his game.

"Third graders think they're tough," Madeline said.

Joey agreed. He couldn't believe Madeline had talked back to Eddie, just like that. The same way she told Ronald off. Joey wondered what Madeline would do if Ronald took her candy.

The bell rang and recess was over.

"We invented a new game," Joey said as he and Madeline and Christopher walked toward the door.

"We could call it Pong-Thunk," Madeline said.

"If you miss, you don't get a thunk," Joey said. "But if you catch it, you get to throw it until you miss. The one with the most thunks wins."

Their game had rules and everything. Joey couldn't wait to play again tomorrow.

Chapter
· 10 ·

Thursday. Today was the day Joey was supposed to walk home from school with Madeline. He pushed his scrambled eggs around the plate.

"I guess they're a little watery," Mom said. "Try to eat some."

What if Madeline got sick and didn't come to school, Joey wondered. He'd have to walk home alone.

As Joey walked into the schoolyard, he heard Christopher call, "Joey, wait up." Joey stopped and let Christopher catch up. "Madeline brought a tennis ball," Christopher told him. "So did I. Want to play Pong-Thunk at lunch? We could get some more kids."

"Sure," said Joey.

"Hey, King," Ronald called. "Found your Prince Charming?"

Christopher turned red. He looked down and walked quickly ahead of Joey.

That dumb Ronald, Joey thought. He felt too angry to be embarrassed. First Ronald took his Milky Way. Now he'd made Christopher feel embarrassed. Pretty soon, Joey thought, he wasn't going to have any friends. Everyone would be afraid to be seen with him. Why did his name have to be King? Why wouldn't Ronald leave him alone?

Mrs. Sullivan took attendance. Then she said, "Today we're going to play a game for our reading lesson." Some kids cheered.

"Let's play the harmonica," Ronald said.

"Only when we have extra time," Mrs. Sullivan said. "And that's another check for speaking out of turn, Mr. Boyd."

Joey hoped this game would teach him how to read. But he didn't see how playing a game was going to help. He wondered if the substitute folder said to play a game.

Mrs. Sullivan divided the class into two

teams, down the middle of the room. Three rows on one side. Three on the other.

"Let's see which team can think of the most words to rhyme with this word," she said. She wrote a word on the board and spelled it out loud. "S-i-n-g." She wrote it twice and underlined it. Once on one side of the board, and again on the other side, for team one and team two. "Who knows what word this is?"

Madeline raised her hand. No one else did. How come Madeline thought she knew that word, Joey wondered. She could hardly even see. How could she read? Maybe she would be wrong. Ronald would say something stupid. Everyone would laugh.

"Madeline," Mrs. Sullivan said.

"The word is *sing*," Madeline told her.

"Good," Mrs. Sullivan said. "Now, what rhymes with *sing?*"

Madeline raised her hand. So did some other kids. Joey knew a word that rhymed, but he didn't raise his hand. He looked at his desk and hoped Ronald wouldn't think of it.

"Ring," said Christopher.

"Thing," said Madeline.

"Bring," said Jonathan.

"Sting," said Mary Jane.

Mrs. Sullivan wrote the words down. "Good," she said. "Anyone else? That's two and two."

Ronald put his head on his desk and started to laugh.

"King," he said in a muffled voice. Then he looked up. "King," he said loudly and pointed at Joey. Joey felt as if a hundred eyes were looking at him.

"That's two to three," Mrs. Sullivan said. "Looks like Ronald's side of the room wins." We win because Ronald has a big mouth, Joey thought. Looks like the name King is good for something. If only it was someone else's name! Joey wished he were on the other side of the room, even if they did lose.

◇

In music class, Madeline knew all the answers again.

"Showoff," Ronald whispered. "Four-eyes is a showoff."

Joey looked out the window. He wondered if Madeline had heard. Maybe she didn't care. She kept raising her hand. How come Madeline knew all the answers?

Joey watched the light at the corner turn green. That's the light where Madeline and I cross, Joey thought. At least I think it's the light. It was hard to tell from inside on the second floor of the school building. Joey got twisted around in his directions sometimes. He wished Daniel didn't have to stay for intramurals.

After music it was time to line up before going home. Madeline was at the front of the room, but Joey got stuck near the back. They should have picked a place to meet, Joey thought. But when he got outside and looked around, Madeline was right next to him. At least he didn't have to find her.

"Let's go," Madeline said. She started to walk down toward the light. Joey followed.

"Hey," Ronald yelled after them. "The king found a queen. There goes the king with four-eyes." Joey just kept walking. He didn't look back. He wished he could sink through the sidewalk.

"Ronald's even worse without Mrs. Fulks here," Madeline said.

Joey agreed, but he didn't feel like talking about it.

"He stayed back," Madeline went on. "He's supposed to be in second grade."

"How do you know?" Joey asked.

"My sister knows his sister. She told me. They moved here this summer."

"That's why he looks so big," Joey said.

"I bet he was kept back for being so mean," Madeline added. She looked up at the big letters on the street sign. "Linden Avenue," she read.

"You can't read that," Joey told her. "You just know the name of this street."

"I know the name of this street, *and* I can read it," Madeline said.

Joey felt angry. He didn't believe Madeline could read and he couldn't. He felt like saying, "But you can't even see."

Instead he said, "Prove it. Read that sign." He pointed to the huge letters on the window of a store where he and Daniel went to buy candy sometimes after school.

Madeline walked up close to the window and squinted. She moved her head from one side to the other as she read each line.

"Wilkins Market. Fine foods. Open seven days a week."

Joey knew it was Wilkins Market, but he didn't know the sign said that other stuff.

"Where did you learn how to read?" he asked Madeline. "How did you know the word *sing* in reading today?"

"I have a home tutor," Madeline explained. "Because I have so much trouble seeing. I have to do extra schoolwork so I won't get behind, or else I can't stay in this school."

Joey didn't want to do extra schoolwork, but he sure wanted to read. "I wish I could read," he said.

"It's easy," Madeline told him. "Just like the rhyming game we played today. Start with the word *an.* Then add another letter like p. Sound it out. P-an. Pan. Fan. Can."

"Do you have special help in music too?" Joey asked.

"I have piano lessons," Madeline said. "Blind people are good at listening."

"But you aren't blind," said Joey.

"The doctors say I might be someday if my eyes keep getting worse."

Joey thought being blind would be awful. He wondered if it would be like walking around in the dark all the time. It was too scary to think about.

"Here comes the king. Here comes the queen." It was Eddie across the street at the corner, singing. There were some other kids there too. Joey hoped they wouldn't wait for him and Madeline. He hoped they would keep walking.

Joey and Madeline waited for the light to change. Joey wished for the hundredth time that he could change his name. Maybe he could. His whole family could. That would sure solve some problems. Then no one would notice him.

The big kids were walking away. The light changed. Joey walked slowly, a little behind Madeline. He could see his street now. He knew exactly where he was. Madeline's was the next street up. Getting home without Daniel wasn't so bad.

"Bye," Joey said to Madeline at the corner of his street.

"Bye," Madeline said. "Maybe we can play Pong-Thunk again tomorrow."

"Sure," Joey said, but he had other things on his mind besides Pong-Thunk.

Chapter
· 11 ·

Joey walked down the block toward his house. He was thinking of names. "Joey Linden, Joey Wilkins." He tried them out loud. His new name had to be simple. King was simple. But Joey needed a simple name that didn't mean anything. And he had to be able to spell it. He liked Fulks, but that was Mrs. Fulks' name. Brown was an easy last name but that was a color. Joey Fulks, Joey Brown. They sounded pretty good.

As Joey walked up the driveway, he saw the red two-door parked in front of the garage. Dad's car. The Toyota. Joey Toyota, Joey tried. No, he thought. Everyone knows Toyota is a car.

Dad taught at the university and on

Thursdays he didn't have any afternoon classes. Joey raced up the back steps and threw his backpack on the kitchen table. Sometimes on his half-day Dad played soccer with Joey and Daniel.

"Dad! Hey, Dad," Joey called on his way up the stairs.

"In here." He heard his father's voice from the study.

Joey opened the door.

"What's up?" Dad asked. He was typing.

Joey leaned against the arm of his dad's chair.

"I was wondering," Joey began. "Does anyone ever change their name?"

"Sometimes," Dad said. "I remember when I was about your age I had a friend named William Williams. Imagine giving someone the same first and last name."

Imagine giving someone the name King, Joey wanted to say.

"The kids used to call my friend Wee Willy Willy," Dad continued. "Boy, he hated that. You can imagine."

"I can imagine," Joey said. "So what did he do?"

"He learned how to fight," Dad said. "By the time he was in third grade, no one messed with him. When he was in high school he used his middle name, Bradley. Brad Williams."

Joey thought about his middle name: Emery, after his grandfather. Joseph Emery. He didn't think Emery was such a great middle name. But now that he thought about it, it sounded like a good last name.

"Does anyone ever change their last name?" Joey asked.

"Your mom changed her name when we got married," Dad said.

That's right, Joey remembered. Grandma and Grandpa Elliot were Mom's mother and father. Elliot wasn't a bad name. Too bad Dad didn't change his name instead.

"Some people had their names changed when they came to this country. The immigration people couldn't pronounce or spell their real names so they gave them new ones. Just like that. It's a shame, really," Dad said. "A person's name is important. It's part of his heritage. Now, what's all this about changing names? Is someone you know changing his name?"

"Well," Joey said, "I was thinking maybe we could change our name. Elliot isn't bad. It was Mom's name."

"Gee," Dad said, "if I changed my name now, no one would know who I was. It wouldn't be very good for business."

"Why?" Joey asked.

"If I started putting a new name on all these papers I write, everyone would say, 'Who is this guy Elliot?' Besides, King's not such a bad name," Dad said. "It's short and easy to spell. And," he added, laughing, "I kind of like being a king."

"Did anyone ever tease you about your name?" Joey asked.

"Not that I remember. Is someone teasing you?"

"Yes," said Joey. "All the time." Joey figured if he didn't tell Dad who was teasing, he wasn't really tattling.

"I don't think changing your name will help much," Dad said. "Kids who want to tease will usually find something to tease about, no matter what it is. If it wasn't your name it would be something else. Try to ignore it. Is there something I can do to help? I could speak to your teacher or . . ."

"No," Joey said quickly. It looked like Dad wasn't big on changing names. Ronald was going to be teasing him forever.

Dad started typing again. "How about kicking the soccer ball around when I'm done?"

"Sure," Joey said.

Joey went into his room and climbed onto his bed. He thought about the name King. Then he thought about the rhyming game they had played in school. King, sing, thing. He even thought of some more words. Fling, sling. Then Joey thought about some other words that rhymed. Pet, bet, set. He climbed off his bed and went to his desk. He took some paper and folded it together to make some pages like a book.

At the top of the first page Joey wrote *pet.* Then he wrote *S* under it. He sounded it out the way Madeline had said. *Set.* He wrote *M* and sounded out *met. L* made *Let.*

Joey looked at the page. At the bottom of the page he wrote, Let pet set. He read it to himself. He was reading! Wow, Joey thought, I can read!

He went over to Daniel's bookcase and took down a book with a rabbit on the cover, a book Daniel liked a lot. Daniel had read it three times. Joey opened the cover and looked at the words. There were too many of them. He couldn't make anything out. Joey closed the book and put it back. He was never going to be able to read like Daniel.

He went back to his desk. Let pet set. He could read that. Joey turned the page and began to write some more words. Get, bet. I'm reading, Joey thought. I *can* read.

He was going to make a whole book. Then he would read it to Mom and Dad. Who needs first grade, Joey thought. He was reading, and he taught himself.

At dinner that night, Joey wanted to tell about the book he was making, but he thought Daniel would laugh. Instead, he listened as Daniel told about a book he was reading in school.

"It was about a man named Gandhi in India," Daniel told the family. "He went on a hunger strike. He stopped eating and told the people in his country that he wouldn't eat again unless they stopped fighting and killing each other."

"Did it work?" Joey asked.

"In a way it did. Even though there was still fighting, many people stopped and began listening to Gandhi. They didn't want him to die."

If he stopped eating, Joey thought, maybe he could get his family to change their name.

"Gandhi was a very brave man," Dad said. "There are only a few people in this world who can truly stand up for what they believe and be willing to die for it."

I could go on a hunger strike, Joey thought. We could change our name to Gandhi.

"I don't think I could be that brave," Daniel said.

Joey Gandhi. Joey didn't think that sounded quite right.

"I don't know if I could give my life for a cause either," Dad said. "But sometimes we don't find out until what we really believe in is challenged."

"What do you mean?" Daniel asked.

"There may be a time when you see something so terrible happening to yourself or your family or your country that you have no choice but to do something about it even if it is very dangerous."

"Joseph." Mother interrupted Joey's thoughts about what Daniel and Dad were saying. "Eat the rest of your dinner or no dessert."

Joseph Gandhi sounded better than Joey Gandhi. With such an important name, Joseph sounded better. Joey wondered if Gandhi had given up dessert when he stopped eating.

◇

"Pick a bedtime story," Dad said to Joey, later that evening.

"Here's a new one," Joey said. "I made it and I can read it."

"OK," Dad said. "You read it to me."

Joey read his book to Dad. "Get pet. Let pet set. Bet pet. Get bet."

"I'm impressed," Dad said. "Mom would like to hear this too."

Joey read his book again for Mom.

That night in bed, Joey thought about what his father had said at dinner. He said it was brave to stand up for your rights. Dad's friend had to learn how to fight when kids teased him. Joey knew he would get into trouble if he tried to fight with Ronald. He was afraid to do that. Ronald was big.

Joey wasn't brave like Gandhi. But it was wrong for Ronald to tease him and Madeline all the time. Gandhi would have known how to make Ronald stop being mean without fighting.

Joey was going to do something about it, only he didn't know what. He wished he were in third grade and that he could read. Then he could read the book about Gandhi.

But I *can* read, Joey thought. He remembered his book and stretched his toes out straight to the bottom of his bed. He could read his own book and tomorrow he was going to write more.

Chapter
• 12 •

Joey was getting dressed for school on Friday. "Here, you can have this," Daniel said. He tossed the purple spider shirt over to Joey. "Mom's right. It doesn't fit me anymore." Daniel looked sad.

Joey liked that shirt, but he didn't want to take it away from Daniel. "Maybe you should keep it anyway," Joey told him. "It still fits a little."

"No," Daniel said. "I wore that shirt in first grade. You're lucky. You're in first grade and it fits you." Daniel slumped down on his bed. "In first grade everything is easy."

"I don't think so," Joey said.

"Shows what you know," Daniel said. "In first grade you get to play T-ball instead of baseball in gym, homework takes about five minutes, and you get to print instead of write cursive. You may as well have the shirt too."

"Yeah," Joey agreed. He didn't know what else to say. Maybe third grade wasn't so great. "Do you wish you were still in first grade?"

"Sometimes," Daniel said. "When we play baseball or have to write cursive." He left the room and went downstairs.

"Thanks for the shirt," Joey called after him. He pulled off his striped shirt and pulled the purple one on. It felt great.

Joey loved gym class and T-ball. He liked making straight lines and neat circles that reached the upper case and lower case guidelines. Maybe first grade *was* better than third, Joey thought. But he still didn't know what to do about Ronald.

◇

Mrs. Sullivan flicked the lights for everyone's attention. "It's time to line up for art class," she said.

"We're supposed to go to the bathroom first," Ronald called out without even raising his hand.

"We are already late, so if you need to use

the bathroom, you can just ask Mr. Russell." Ronald made a face and some kids laughed. No one told Mrs. Sullivan that Mr. Russell didn't let kids go to the bathroom.

Madeline was in line in front of Joey. "Mr. Russell is mean," she whispered. "I hate art. I'm terrible at it."

"It's not so bad," Joey told her. "Hey, I made a book of rhyming words. I sounded out the words, like you said. It works."

"Quiet in the back of the line," Mrs. Sullivan said in her crackly voice. Madeline turned bright red. She quickly faced forward.

Joey stood up straight, looking at the back of Madeline's head.

"It's the king and queen." Ronald snickered.

"Madeline, Joey, and Ronald," Mrs. Sullivan said sternly, "checks for all of you."

Why couldn't that kid keep quiet? Joey felt his face turn hot. He knew it was red. Mrs. Fulks was going to think he was really a troublemaker when she came back, all because of Ronald. Ronald didn't even care about checks.

In art class they had to walk in a line to their seats around two big work tables. That meant Madeline ended up next to Joey. There was a large piece of paper at each place.

"Sit down and fold your hands," Mr. Russell said. "And no talking. Today I want you to draw a picture with crayons."

"Not again." Ronald groaned.

Mr. Russell stared at him for a whole minute. Ronald slid down in his seat. "That will be enough," Mr. Russell told him.

Joey sat up straight with his hands folded. He kept his eyes on his paper.

Mr. Russell continued giving directions. "Next week we will cover the picture with water paint. This is called a crayon resist. Now get to work. You get only one piece of paper, so if you mess it up you have no project for two weeks."

Joey looked at the crayons. The crayons were all in order. Everything was so neat. The paper was straight. The table was clean.

Madeline was swinging her feet under the table. Joey wished she would stop. She just sat there swinging her feet and didn't start to draw. Joey couldn't stand it.

"Stop shaking the chair," he whispered.

"I can't draw anything," Madeline said.

She looked at Joey. She's going to cry, Joey thought, any minute.

Joey looked at his own paper. It was so big and clean and white. Joey was afraid to make a mark.

He thought maybe he could make a dog. Daniel made great dogs. He was an artist. If only Joey could remember how Daniel did it.

Other kids were working. Joey could see Christopher bent over his paper. He was using a blue crayon. Joey was afraid he would start in the wrong place or maybe make the dog too little. He always did that.

"I have to go to the bathroom," Ronald called out. Kids giggled.

"That's not the way to ask," Mr. Russell said. He was walking around the room looking at the pictures. "You can wait until after this class."

He was getting closer to Joey and Madeline. "Fill up more of your paper," he said to Christopher.

Joey still hadn't started. Madeline picked up the box of crayons and held it close to her face.

"Madeline must be color blind too," Ronald mumbled. Mr. Russell would sure let Ronald have it if he heard that, Joey thought. But Mr. Russell hadn't heard.

He was getting closer and Joey knew he had to do something about his empty paper. "Just jump in," Dad always said. Joey thought about jumping in. He liked to jump into leaf piles, and snow, and water. Water in the pool and water in the lake. He picked up a blue crayon and made a bumpy line for water.

Oh, no, Joey thought. The line was purple, not blue, and he had made it too close to the top of the paper. Joey looked at his paper. Mr. Russell was almost behind him. Joey turned the paper around. Now the purple line was near the bottom. He made more bumpy lines, blue and green. All water colors. Then Joey made a red rectangle for a boat. This was going to be a great picture. He drew two red triangles for sails. Joey made good triangles.

Mr. Russell was next to him now. "That's fine water," Mr. Russell said. "I like that."

Joey nodded his head. He didn't say anything but he felt good.

Suddenly Madeline made a strange noise. Joey looked at her.

"Oh, no," she groaned. Then she put her

head down on the paper. Her shoulders were shaking.

Crying, Joey thought. Because she can't draw anything and Mr. Russell is getting close. Then Joey heard something else. He sat still and listened. He thought for a minute. Then he looked down. Under Madeline's chair. It looked like there was a puddle. A puddle right there on the floor. It was starting to make a river, and the river was starting to spread under Joey's chair. Joey wanted to jump up out of the way, but Mr. Russell was standing behind him. Joey pulled his legs up and crossed them on his chair.

Chapter
· 13 ·

Joey couldn't believe his eyes. He looked at Madeline. Her head was still on the table. Now she was really crying. He didn't blame her.

"Madeline, please sit up and get to work," Mr. Russell said crossly. He was standing behind Joey and Madeline now.

"She's crying," Mary Jane said.

"Madeline," Mr. Russell said, "pick your head up and tell me why you are crying. It is impossible for me to help you unless you tell me what is the matter." He sounded angry now. Everyone was looking at Madeline. She raised her head but she didn't say anything. Joey didn't say anything either.

"Madeline, you are disrupting the class and . . ." Mr. Russell stopped talking. He was looking down at the floor. He was looking at his feet. The puddle under Madeline's chair was creeping over to Mr. Russell's shoes.

"What . . ." Mr. Russell began, then he stopped again. He made a funny face. "Who will take Madeline to the nurse?" he asked.

"What's wrong with Madeline?" Mary Jane and Christopher and Jonathan and Sara were all looking under the table. "Ooooooo." "She wet her pants." Kids were whispering and making faces. There was some giggling. "Eeuuuuuu." "Yuk." "It's on the floor."

"Who knows where the nurse's office is?" Mr. Russell asked.

No one answered.

Joey knew where the nurse's office was, but he kept quiet. He looked at Madeline. Her eyes were red and puffy. Her nose was running. Mr. Russell was getting angry. Why didn't someone do something?

Joey couldn't stand it. He raised his hand slowly.

"Thank you, Joey," Mr. Russell said. "Please tell the nurse we need a custodian here."

Joey stepped around the puddle.

Madeline stood up. Her dress was dripping in back.

"The king to the rescue," Joey heard Ronald say as Mr. Russell led them to the door. "Better get four-eyes to the nurse before she drowns." Joey heard giggles. Then Mr. Russell closed the door behind them.

It wasn't fair. Why didn't Mr. Russell send Ronald to the office? Instead, it was Joey going to the nurse with Madeline, and Ronald was making fun of them. If Mrs. Fulks had been there, she wouldn't have let this happen. Mrs. Fulks knew how to handle Ronald, and she would have let everyone go to the bathroom before art class.

◇

Joey walked back to art class on his own. He wished he could have stayed at the nurse's office with Madeline.

"Well, Mr. King, what are you doing out here in the hall by yourself?" Joey jumped. It was Mrs. Sullivan. Now what was he going to do? How could he explain about Madeline?

Mrs. Sullivan didn't have her yardstick,

and her arms were full of books and papers. Joey figured he could run away, right out the school door, if he had to.

"Wandering in the halls is against the school rules," Mrs. Sullivan reminded him. "Speak up, or I'll have to keep you after school."

Joey knew he had to explain. Why should he get blamed when it was Madeline who wet her pants? It wasn't fair. Ronald never got in trouble, but he, Joey, might have to stay after school for nothing.

"I had to take Madeline to the nurse's office," Joey began. He kept talking until he had told Mrs. Sullivan the whole story. It just came out.

Mrs. Sullivan's mouth made a straight line. "Thank you, Joey," she said quietly. "It looks like I'd better allow more time for the class to go to the bathroom."

Joey nodded his head. Mrs. Sullivan looked annoyed, but Joey didn't think she was mad at him.

"Is there anything else I should know about your class while Mrs. Fulks is away?" she asked.

Joey looked at her in surprise. Should he

tell Mrs. Sullivan about Ronald? That would be tattling, and Daniel had said he'd get into trouble for that. Maybe he should keep quiet and mind his own business. It was last period and they would go home soon.

But who knew how much longer Mrs. Fulks would be away? Besides, this *was* Joey's business. Someone like Gandhi wouldn't have kept quiet. He would have done something. Ronald was making life miserable for Joey and for Madeline, and for anyone who wanted to be Joey's friend.

"There must be something I should know," Mrs. Sullivan said. She was staring right at Joey. He could practically feel her eyes.

Joey's mouth was dry, but Mrs. Sullivan had asked him and she was waiting.

"No," he said. "I mean yes." Then he began. He told Mrs. Sullivan all about how Ronald teased him and Madeline. He said he didn't think it was right for Ronald to make fun of Madeline's eyes. He said maybe it would be worse from now on. Ronald was sure to make fun of Madeline for wetting her pants and Joey for taking her to the nurse. He even told Mrs. Sullivan that he thought Ronald stole his Milky Way but he couldn't prove it.

Maybe Daniel would call him a tattletale, but Joey thought he was standing up for his rights and Madeline's too.

"Thank you for telling me," Mrs. Sullivan said again. "Now you come back to the room and get ready to go home. Art class is almost over. Your classmates will be back soon."

Joey couldn't tell if Mrs. Sullivan was mad or not. He probably should have kept his mouth shut. What if she got real mad at Ronald? What if she said, "Joey King told me you stole his candy bar"? He hadn't said that, but what if Mrs. Sullivan told Ronald he had?

When the class came back from art, all Mrs. Sullivan said was, "Get your coats and line up."

"Hey, King, did the queen make it to the potty?" Ronald whispered on the way back to his seat. Joey looked over at Mrs. Sullivan, but she hadn't noticed. She'd probably forgotten the whole thing.

Lucky for me, Joey thought. Now he didn't know which would be worse, putting up with Ronald's teasing or having Ronald and the other kids find out Joey had tattled. Either way would be bad. Joey wanted to get out of school. He wished the line would move faster.

"Joey?" It was Madeline. She was practically on top of him. "Can I walk home with you? I don't want Molly to know what happened." They were out in front of the school. "The nurse let me wait until the class left the room to get my things."

Joey just started walking. He saw Daniel and Brian come out the third grade door. He wanted to keep up with them. He didn't want Madeline to walk with him but he didn't want to say no.

"It's lucky Miss Gilbert keeps extra clothes around for times like this," Madeline went on. "These are my wet things." She held up a brown paper bag. "I have to bring hers back tomorrow. She says it happens all the time."

Joey didn't say anything. He was glad it hadn't happened to him.

"Did you go back to art class?" Madeline asked after they crossed Linden Avenue.

"No," Joey said. "Mrs. Sullivan saw me in

the hall. I thought I was going to get it. But I didn't, and I ended up telling her all about Ronald and how mean he is and everything."

"You did?" Madeline stopped walking. "Boy, are you in trouble if he finds out."

Joey didn't answer her. Madeline was quiet for a minute. Then she said, "Thanks. Thanks for going to the nurse with me."

Joey shrugged.

"Maybe Mrs. Sullivan won't say anything," Madeline said. "She can't stop Ronald anyway. It's just bad luck he had to repeat first grade and be in our class."

Joey didn't feel like talking about it.

"See you tomorrow," Madeline said as Joey turned down his street.

Madeline was right. What made him think he could change things anyway? But Joey was mad. He was tired of putting up with Ronald.

Now I'm a tattletale, Joey thought, but that's not going to help. I'll have to fight back like Dad said. Not the way Dad meant, though.

Madeline had said Ronald was supposed

to be in second grade. Joey was going to make him wish he were. He had the whole weekend to think of a way to get even with Ronald.

Chapter
· 14 ·

It was Monday and Joey had a plan. He got up extra early and got dressed. Daniel was still asleep. "Hey, Dan," Joey asked, "how do you spell *repeater?*"

Daniel groaned. "Turn out the light."

"OK," Joey said, "but tell me."

"R-E-P-E-A-T-E-R," came from under the covers. Joey wrote it neatly on a white piece of paper. He was going to get Ronald back. Ronald the repeater. It was so simple. By lunchtime everyone in the class would know Ronald was a repeater.

◇

"Everyone put your books and papers away," Mrs. Sullivan said after she took attendance. "Today we are going to do something different."

"Are you going to play the harmonica?" Mary Jane asked.

"Not today," Mrs. Sullivan said. She didn't smile.

Oh no, Joey thought. Mrs. Sullivan was going to spoil his plan. She was going to tell the class what had happened. Ronald would let him have it good and the whole school would know he was a tattletale.

"We are going to play a game," Mrs. Sullivan said. "It is a game about trust. We are going to need partners for this activity, so as I count off—one, two—I want you to go get your coats and get in line next to your partners. We'll go outside where we have more room."

Oh brother, Joey thought. The last thing he felt like doing was playing a game. He just wanted school to be over. Forget about Ronald. Forget about his plan.

"One, two. One, two," Mrs. Sullivan counted off. The kids lined up. "One," she said pointing to Ronald. "Two" was Joey.

What does she think she's doing? Joey

wondered. Maybe this was a punishment. He knew he should never have told Mrs. Sullivan anything. How could he and Ronald be partners? Joey looked around. Madeline was partners with Mary Jane. Christopher had gotten Tim. Joey felt miserable.

"I got the king," Ronald announced as the class moved outside. "It's me and the king."

Oh brother, Joey thought.

Outside, Mrs. Sullivan passed out strips of cloth. "These are blindfolds," she said. "One for each pair of partners."

She explained the game. First the number ones were going to put on the blindfolds and the number twos were going to lead them around the playground, helping them and telling them where to go because they wouldn't be able to see. Then it would be the twos' turn to wear the blindfolds.

"When everyone has had a turn to be blindfolded, we will talk about what it was like," Mrs. Sullivan finished.

Joey couldn't believe it. Was he really supposed to let Ronald lead him around blindfolded? Ronald would probably trip him, or push him off a cliff, or lead him in front of a school bus. Joey thought maybe he could go to the bathroom and hide there. Or maybe to the nurse's office.

At least Ronald had to wear the blindfold first. Joey looked around for him. He couldn't see Ronald anywhere.

All the other kids were getting started. Some were giggling and laughing. Joey saw Christopher head right for the jungle gym but Tim moved him gently away. Joey was the only one standing still.

"Where's your partner?" Mrs. Sullivan asked.

"I can't find him," Joey told her. Maybe he was going to be lucky and Ronald would stay lost, he thought.

"Over here, Joey. Here is Ronald," Mrs. Sullivan called from the edge of the parking lot.

No such luck, Joey thought as he walked over to the parking lot. Ronald was hidden by a big blue station wagon. He was sitting on the curb, holding the blindfold.

"Stand up," Mrs. Sullivan told Ronald. He shook his head. Mrs. Sullivan reached for the blindfold. Ronald grabbed it back.

"Joey is waiting," she told Ronald calmly. "You're ruining his chance."

Some chance, Joey thought.

A few of the other kids were slowly coming over to where Ronald and Mrs. Sullivan and Joey were. Suddenly, Ronald jumped up. He threw the blindfold down and stamped on it. "You can't make me," he yelled at the teacher. "I'm not putting that thing on. I'm not, I'm not. The king will probably lead me into a tree or trip me on purpose. He hates me." Ronald started to cry. His face was real red.

Joey couldn't believe it. Ronald was afraid—afraid of him, Joey King! What a joke!

"I know he hates me," Ronald cried. "Everyone in this class hates me." By now a whole group of kids had gathered around Ronald. Some had taken off their blindfolds. No one said a word.

"I'm very sorry you feel that way," Mrs. Sullivan said to Ronald. "I'm sure your classmates don't hate you."

A few kids shook their heads and some mumbled, "No, we don't," but Joey could tell the others were as surprised as he was.

Ronald the Repeater was afraid. Afraid to let Joey lead him.

Mrs. Sullivan picked up the blindfold. "Joey isn't going to hurt you, Ronald. I'll help tie the blindfold on for you."

"No," Ronald yelled again. He grabbed the blindfold. "You can't make me." He was twisting the blindfold around and around in his hands.

"Perhaps Joey would go first?" Mrs. Sullivan turned to Joey, making it a question.

"I bet he won't," Ronald said as he wiped a tear. He had stopped crying and there was a dirt smudge on his face. He still sounded angry. Joey almost felt sorry for him. That's something Joey never wanted to do, cry in front of the whole class. He also did not want to go first. For that matter, he did not want to go at all, not with Ronald for a partner.

"What do you say, Joey?" Mrs. Sullivan was waiting. The whole class was waiting.

"I'll go first," Joey said quietly.

With the blindfold on, Joey took short steps. His toe hit a ridge and he knew he had

gone from the smooth blacktop to the bumpy grass area. Everything felt closed in and empty at the same time. The blindfold tickled his nose. Joey wanted to reach up and adjust it so he could peek.

Ronald was holding his arm to guide him. "Hey, King, where're you going? That's the swing you're trying to walk into." Ronald pulled Joey over to the right. Joey moved slowly, sliding one foot in front of the other.

"How come you went first?" Ronald asked. "Mrs. Sullivan wouldn't have made you."

"I don't know," Joey said. "Someone had to, I guess." With each step Joey felt he was going to bump into something. He held one arm straight out in front as he moved. His feet told him he was on the hard asphalt again.

"You don't want to go up the steps," Ronald said as he turned Joey around.

Joey started to move a little faster but he still kept his arm out in front. "You want a turn now?" he asked Ronald. "I won't try anything."

"I know you won't," Ronald said. "You'd be too scared."

Joey thought about it. Is that why he

didn't like to do mean things? Because he was too scared?

He took off the blindfold and handed it to Ronald. "No," he said. "I just wouldn't."

"Well," Ronald said, "I'll try for a minute. Mrs. Sullivan will make me anyway." He put the blindfold on.

Joey took his hand and started to walk, but he pulled back. "Trust me," Joey said. He led Ronald back toward Mrs. Sullivan. Ronald took little baby steps the whole way. Joey could tell he was really afraid, but he kept the blindfold on until Mrs. Sullivan said it was time to end the game.

Ronald the Repeater was afraid! Joey was glad he wasn't afraid like that. And he was glad he hadn't had time to put his plan to work. It didn't seem like such a good idea anymore. It seemed kind of dumb. He felt bad that he even thought of it.

Back in the classroom, Mrs. Sullivan asked the class to talk about what it had been like to be blind and to be the leader.

Mary Jane said, "It was fun." Tim said being the leader was hard work.

"I think being blindfolded was scary," Christopher said.

"Me too." Most of the class agreed.

Sara raised her hand. "I want to know if Madeline feels like that all the time, scared because she can't see some things."

"It's different," Madeline said. "Usually I'm not scared. But sometimes I am, when I can't understand directions and I don't know what to do, or when I don't know where things are or who people are."

Ronald raised his hand. "I think the king was brave to let me lead him," he said. Ronald called Joey "the king," but no one laughed. "The king" almost sounded important, the way he said it.

Making sure no one was watching, Joey opened his desk. Carefully, he slipped a piece of paper out of his reading workbook. It was a sign. It said RONALD THE REPEATER. He had planned to stick the sign on Ronald's desk. Then he was going to tell everybody, Mary Jane and Christopher and Jonathan and Sally, that Ronald was a repeater. Now he was glad he hadn't. With his hands inside the closed desk, Joey ripped the paper into tiny pieces.

Chapter
• 15 •

"Mrs. Fulks has to stay away a few more days," Mrs. Sullivan announced to the class on Tuesday morning. "Her father is doing a little better and she'll be back next Monday." She took the chart down. "I think first graders know how to behave without checks. Mrs. Fulks doesn't need to see these." She smiled and winked at Joey. Joey smiled too.

Mrs. Sullivan stuffed the chart into the wastebasket by her desk. Joey was glad he didn't have to worry about checks anymore.

"I think we should plan for a party for Friday," Mrs. Sullivan continued. The class cheered. "I'll play the harmonica, and maybe some of you can volunteer to bring the treats."

Later, Joey's team won the rhyming

game. Ronald stuck his hand out at Joey. Joey slapped him five. "Way to go, King," Ronald said.

At lunch time a lot of the boys and girls were standing around watching Joey and Christopher and Madeline play Pong-Thunk. "Yea, Madeline," the girls cheered when Madeline got a thunk. Mary Jane and Jonathan asked if they could play. Even Daniel and Brian took a few turns.

"Pretty good catch," Brian told Joey when he caught a thunk.

On Wednesday, Joey walked home with Madeline even though it wasn't an intramurals day. When they passed the market, they met Eddie and some of his friends coming out the door.

"Make way for the king and queen," they jeered and laughed. Then they ran ahead to make the light. Joey and Madeline kept walking slowly.

"Molly says Eddie has a big mouth sometimes," Madeline said.

"I think she's right," Joey agreed.

"Ronald is being pretty nice, though," Madeline added. "He hasn't said anything mean all week."

"I think he wants to be friends," Joey said.

"Maybe we could ask him to play Pong-Thunk at lunch tomorrow."

"Sure," Joey said. "That's a great idea."

The next day, Mrs. Sullivan handed out reading books. She told the class to take them home and read them for homework. Joey couldn't wait. Finally, a book! It was paper and real skinny, only twenty-nine pages with big print, but it was a real book and he could read it.

As soon as he got home, Joey got up on his bunk bed and began to read. "See the deer eat meat. Heat the meat." Joey looked at the picture. It was funny. A deer sat by a campfire cooking a hot dog on a stick. Joey kept reading until he finished the whole book. Some of the words he didn't know, but he sounded them out like Madeline had told him to do, and then he could read them. He felt great.

At dinner, when everyone had finished eating, Joey read his book to the family. "Bravo," Dad said. He and Mom both clapped. Daniel didn't do anything. At least he didn't make fun of the easy book, Joey thought. And now Joey had proof that he could read.

"I'd like to hear that one more time," Dad said.

Joey read his book again. He was surprised when Daniel said, "I remember reading that. You learned fast. You've only been in first grade a few weeks."

Joey smiled.

"You should try some of my books," Daniel told him.

"Thanks," Joey said.

"Wait until Mrs. Fulks hears how well you read when she comes back," Mom said.

"We're having a party tomorrow for Mrs. Sullivan's last day," Joey told his family.

"Lucky first graders," Daniel grumbled. "We never get a party."

"Mrs. Sullivan is going to play the harmonica and we're supposed to bring treats. Could I bring cupcakes?"

"Sure," Mom said. "I think we have all the ingredients. Come on, Joey, if we start now we'll be able to finish them before bedtime. You can help me read the recipe."

Joey was licking the frosting off the beater

when Daniel came into the kitchen. "Want some?" Joey asked. He handed Daniel the other beater.

"Sure," Daniel said. "Thanks." Then he handed Joey a long thin strip of cardboard. "Here. This is for you. It's a bookmark." Daniel had drawn a butterfly on it and there was a gold tassel on one end. "Mom showed me how to make the tassels," he explained.

"Neat," Joey said. "I like the colors on the butterfly. Thanks."

◇

On Friday morning, Mom put the cupcakes in a big flat box.

"I hope this is OK," she said. "If my car weren't in the shop, I would drive you."

Joey was worried about the cupcakes. He and Mom had decorated them. They had white icing with colored sprinkles. He didn't want to drop them.

Daniel helped Joey carry the box to school. When they got there they met Madeline. Joey asked her to carry his lunchbox. He took the cupcakes from Daniel. The box was kind of floppy. Joey held the bottom and walked slowly.

"See you later," Daniel said as he and Brian headed for the third grade doors. "Save some for me."

"Hey," Ronald called. "What's in the box?" He ran over to Joey and Madeline.

"Cupcakes," Madeline told Ronald. "Joey and his mom made them."

"Need some help?" Ronald asked. He put his hands on the box. The cupcakes slid to one side.

"Watch it," Joey told him. He straightened the box.

"Sorry," Ronald said.

"You can take this," Madeline told Ronald. She handed him Joey's lunchbox. They all walked toward the blue doors together.

"What's in the box, King?" someone behind them said.

"Oh, no, not Eddie," Madeline whispered.

"None of your business," Ronald said over his shoulder.

"Who's this?" Eddie asked. He stepped in front of the three first graders and blocked their way. "Aren't you the repeater? Ronald the Repeater?" He laughed.

Ronald didn't answer.

What a big mouth, Joey thought. Pretty

soon everyone in the whole school would hear him. Joey remembered what Daniel had said about Eddie trying to be tough. He's just talk, Daniel had said.

Joey spoke up. "Don't mind him." He hoped he sounded like he didn't care what Eddie did.

"Oh, it's the king." Eddie laughed louder.

"That's right," Joey said. "I'm the king. Make way for the cakes! Come on," he said to Ronald and Madeline. Joey pushed right past Eddie, and Madeline and Ronald followed him to the first grade door.

"Make way for the king," Ronald said, holding the door open for Joey.

After reading, the class made cards for Mrs. Fulks. Joey copied the letters off the board in his neatest printing: WELCOME BACK. Then he wrote his own name. He made a big fancy K for King, and then he drew a design around it. It had a star and two colorful snakes. Not mean snakes, though. Joey liked it. It was his new sign.

Maybe he would make the same fancy K every time he wrote his name. It was special. King wasn't such a bad name.

Joey even felt like a king. He was in first grade, and he could read. He had two new friends, Christopher and Madeline, and it looked like Ronald was going to be his friend too. He and Christopher and Madeline had invented a new game, and everyone wanted to play, even some third graders. And Mrs. Fulks was coming back.

That's right! Joey smiled. A first grade king.